Bella Sara ™

1

Bella's Gift

HarperCollins®, ✿®, and Harper Festival®
are trademarks of HarperCollins Publishers.

Bella Sara: Bella's Gift
Cover and interior illustrations by Heather Theurer.
Copyright © Hidden City Games, Inc. © 2005–2008 conceptcard. All rights reserved.
BELLA SARA is a trademark of conceptcard and is used by Hidden City Games under license.
Licensed by Granada Ventures Limited.
Printed in the United States of America.
For information address HarperCollins Children's Books,
a division of HarperCollins Publishers,
1350 Avenue of the Americas, New York, NY 10019
www.harpercollinschildrens.com
www.bellasara.com

Library of Congress catalog card number: 2008929407
ISBN 978-0-06-167331-3
❖
First Edition

Bella's Gift

Written by Felicity Brown
Illustrated by Heather Theurer

HarperFestival®
A Division of HarperCollinsPublishers

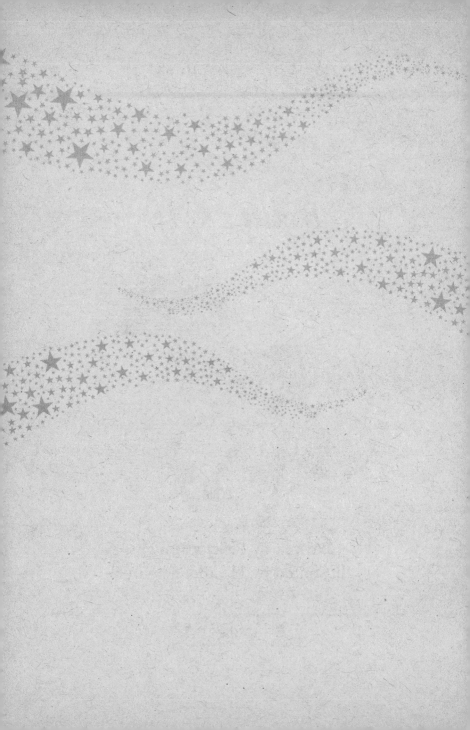

1

It was six o'clock in the evening, and Jillian Frouda was late.

Drifting out of a daydream, Jillian looked around her small stone room. She spotted the tiny tomtomme, whose ringing ears had alerted her to the time.

"Thank you, friend," she said.

The tomtomme nodded back, careful not to disrupt the motion of his tail, which swung in a steady rhythm, ticking off seconds.

Jillian knew she should get moving, but her mind remained fixed on her daydream, which had come to her like a vision. She'd seen a mare with a dazzling white coat that shone like diamonds in sunlight. Her dark eyes, speckled with flecks of gold, were wise and loving. Everything about the horse seemed magical, and Jillian longed to make a drawing of the mare in her memory journal.

Jillian gazed at the pages of the small midnight-blue book lying open on the desk in front of her. This was her most treasured possession. Its worn parchment pages were filled with drawings. Each was a memory of a person or creature Jillian had envisioned in her twelve years.

The visions came to Jillian in flashes, when she was alone and quiet and her mind was free to wander. She was always searching her memory for answers to questions about her past. She tried hard to conjure images of her family, creatures she'd seen, and strangers she had met. By capturing their likenesses in her journal, she felt as if something from her mind were being brought to life, the paper and ink making it real.

Jillian sighed and tucked a stray red curl behind her ear. There was no time now to draw the great horse she'd just seen. Before closing the book, though, she ran her index finger lovingly over the last drawing she had made. *The otter.*

Jillian had seen the otter more than a year ago while she was out in the woods around Styginmoor Castle, collecting berries for her mistress, Ivenna. Down by a small brook, she had felt a strange sensation and turned to see an otter with striking pink fur staring at her, almost as if it was studying her. The creature's gaze was so intense that Jillian had felt suddenly shy and looked away. When she turned back, the otter had disappeared.

The memory of the otter had returned to Jillian—frozen in her mind like an icicle—a week ago. She had eagerly made the drawing, capturing every detail of the animal forever in her journal.

She wondered now if she would see the otter again, as she had so many other creatures she had drawn.

The blank page opposite the illustrated otter beckoned Jillian. But the tomtomme's tail ticked on, a gentle reminder. She had to hurry. It was time to prepare Ivenna's dinner.

It will have to stay blank for now, she thought, as she gently closed the book.

Jillian removed a loose stone from the wall, revealing an empty nook. She tucked the journal, her quill pen, and a small pot of ink into the space and replaced the stone.

As Jillian hurried into the chilly stone corridor, a warm light blossomed in the darkness. A small cave of woven grapevines filled with twinkle imps lit her way. She loved their soft glow, but her heart ached to see them locked up. She wished her tiny friends could be free in the forest, where they belonged.

"I'll sneak you something special from the kitchen," she whispered, careful not to let the wolf guard who was stationed in the corridor overhear. The imps blinked back their thanks.

Jillian had lived within the dank walls of Styginmoor Castle for as long as she could remember. According to Ivenna, the baby Jillian had been abandoned at the gates of Styginmoor by her family, a band of traveling gypsies. She'd had nothing with her but a small satchel containing the midnight-blue leather notebook, a quill pen, and a pot of ink.

Ivenna missed no opportunity to remind Jillian how grateful she should be to have a roof over her head. But life in the castle was difficult. Built on the edge of a marsh near an ancient forest, Styginmoor was not a place of beauty or love. With Ivenna's wolf guards patrolling the castle and its grounds at all times, Jillian was resigned to the fact that she was a prisoner at Styginmoor.

Ivenna presided over the castle with guile and cruelty. She used her army of wolves to frighten the castle's inhabitants into obedience. As her maid, Jillian attended to Ivenna's every whim and need. In all the years Jillian had been at the castle, her mistress had never once spoken a kind word to her. Ivenna trusted no one but her wolf confidante, Myrfor.

Ivenna and Myrfor had always spent hours conspiring and scheming together. Recently, though, their discussions had become even more intense. Jillian had overheard enough to know they were up to something. She didn't know what it was, but she knew it couldn't be good.

Since she received no love from her mistress, the magical creatures who toiled in the castle alongside Jillian had become her family. Like her, some strange fate had led them to Styginmoor, and now they were all trapped there. Jillian dreamed of a life for herself and her magical friends free of the castle's dark, dreary walls and mindless chores.

But even if I could escape, she thought, *I have nothing and no one. Where would I go?*

Jillian rushed through the main kitchen and poked her head anxiously into the dining room. She let out a sigh of relief. Ivenna was not there yet—just some pip-squeak longtails furiously dusting every speck from the large wooden dining table with their long bushy tails.

When the small creatures looked her way, Jillian smiled. "I think you missed a spot," she teased, as she placed a pair of candlesticks on the table.

Back in the kitchen, magical creatures were scurrying around in preparation for the evening meal. Everything

had to be in perfect order before Ivenna and Myrfor arrived.

Bobolinks unloaded heaping baskets of winter berries, mushrooms, and herbs foraged from the forest. Fire spoops were hard at work heating pots of water, and two rose dragons chopped a mound of herbs and vegetables.

The mood in the room seemed to lighten when Jillian entered. "Good evening, friends," she said, taking a particularly heavy basket from a small bobolink and setting it on the counter. She tucked a handful of berries into the pocket of her apron to give to the twinkle imps later.

A large pot of porridge bubbled over an open fire. *Why would Ivenna order porridge for dinner?* Jillian wondered, as she bent to stoke the fire. Ivenna usually ate fancier food.

But as the flames leaped higher, something happened to make her forget about Ivenna's strange request. A form emerged from a bright white flame. It was a horse's head, its mane flaring out behind it.

Jillian was sure her mind was playing tricks on her. First the vision of the magnificent white horse, now this. What could it mean?

But when she stirred the logs again, the horse disappeared.

Just as Jillian was straightening the last piece of silverware on the dining table, she felt a chill trickle down her spine. She didn't have to turn around to know Ivenna and Myrfor had entered the room.

"I see you've left everything to the last minute, as usual." Ivenna's sharp voice echoed off the bare, stone walls.

Jillian turned to see Myrfor sniffing at the air. As usual, his hulking frame, covered in jet-black fur, was tense and rigid. His dark eyes followed her. Not wanting him to sense her fear, Jillian bravely returned his gaze.

Ivenna pointed her metal staff at Jillian and gave her a suspicious look. "I trust you've prepared the meal I requested," she said.

"Yes, of course," Jillian replied. "The porridge will be ready shortly."

"Porridge?" growled Myrfor. He spoke in the language the wolves used to communicate with their riders. It sounded like throaty snarling and snapping. Few humans who were not Wolf Riders could understand it, but Jillian had grown up around Myrfor and his pack.

"Don't worry, Myrfor," Ivenna said. "We won't be eating mush. I ordered the fire spoops to simmer up a joint of meat for us. We will dine as soon as this ridiculous child has served our special guest. Give me the key."

Myrfor bent his neck. Leaning forward, Ivenna lifted off a chain from which hung a massive iron key. She held it out to Jillian. "Take it," she said impatiently when Jillian hesitated.

Jillian swallowed nervously. "What . . . what sort of special guest?" she stammered. Most visitors to the castle were other Wolf Riders, as mysterious and unkind as Ivenna herself.

"That," Ivenna replied, "is for Myrfor and me to know, and for you to find out. But don't worry. I think you'll be rather fond of this guest. It's someone who's rather *drawn* to you already."

Ivenna looked at Myrfor and let out a laugh. Myrfor grinned back at her, his fangs gleaming against his red tongue.

As Jillian turned back toward the kitchen, she felt her stomach clench into a familiar knot of anxiety. Ivenna was a master of cruel games, and surprises around Styginmoor Castle were rarely good.

In all her years at the castle, Jillian had never been in the corridor in which she now found herself. Ivenna had directed her to a secret door in her chambers. It led to a winding set of stairs that went down to a dank, moldy-smelling passage whose walls oozed drops of greenish water. There were no windows, so she couldn't be sure, but Jillian suspected the whole wing was underground.

Jillian followed the turns of the hall cautiously, passing several wolf guards along the way. One of them looked at her and licked his chops. His eyes gleamed red. She tried to steady her shaking hands as the dish of porridge clattered quietly against the heavy silver tray.

"It will be all right," she whispered to herself, only half believing it.

After several minutes, Jillian reached the end of the passage. A small set of stone stairs led up to a thick oak door secured by a heavy iron lock. One thing was certain: Ivenna did not want whoever was inside to get out.

Jillian set the tray carefully on the top stair. Her palms were sweaty as she fumbled in her pocket for the iron key. She recalled how Ivenna had pulled the key from around Myrfor's neck. No doubt it had been with Myrfor for safe-keeping.

Myrfor was the toughest wolf at Styginmoor Castle. No one, human or animal, dared challenge Myrfor, a descendent of Fenrir—the wolf monster who, according to legend, had a power so strong, he could not even be restrained by the gods.

Jillian fitted the key into the lock. Taking a deep breath, she forced herself to turn it swiftly to the left as Ivenna had instructed. With a smooth click, the lock gave way.

Jillian lifted the silver tray once more and pressed open the large oak door with the weight of her body. She immediately felt a presence. A wave of fear washed over her.

Then she saw who was in the room. She gasped with amazement, nearly dropping the tray. *The otter!*

At once, Jillian's fear melted away, replaced with a warm rush of relief. Sensing the creature's goodness, Jillian stepped forward.

"I brought you something to eat," she said, setting the bowl of porridge on a small table. "I'm sorry, it's not much."

Jillian gazed into the otter's big, kind eyes. The otter wore a star-shaped pendant on a chain of pearls around its neck.

"What brought you here . . . to this dark place?" Jillian asked.

The otter looked quickly away, and then back at Jillian. This time Jillian saw a deep sadness in the creature's eyes—and something else as well. Pity.

Puzzled, Jillian cast her eyes downward to the polished silver tray. Her reflection stared back at her.

When she looked up again, Jillian noticed that the stone around the otter's neck was glowing softly. An image flashed into Jillian's mind. The blue journal. She saw herself drawing the otter. Something clicked in her mind.

"*Me?*" Jillian whispered. "Did . . . did . . . did *I* bring you here?"

Jillian knew she'd always had a special bond with animals. Now, standing before the otter, her mind turned to all her magical friends in the castle. As she thought about them, she realized each of them had arrived at Styginmoor soon after she'd drawn them in her notebook. Slowly, things began to make sense. A feeling of dread washed over her.

By drawing them in her journal, Jillian was luring the creatures to the castle. It was *her* fault they had come to Styginmoor and been captured by Ivenna.

A lump formed in Jillian's throat, and a tear splashed down onto the silver tray.

"You are here because of my drawing, aren't you?" she said to the otter. "I am so sorry. I promise you I didn't know." She let out a sob.

Dear child, do not blame yourself. It is true you possess the ability to draw animals to you. This is a rare and special gift, which should be cherished. Instead, it has been abused by your mistress.

The otter could speak to her?

Jillian was so startled, she stopped crying and stared at the creature, her eyes wide with wonder.

It is the Starstone I wear around my neck, explained the otter. *One of its powers is that it allows us to share our thoughts.*

Jillian was fascinated. Her mind filled with questions about the precious Starstone.

I'm afraid there's no time now to tell you more about the stone's magic, said the otter, interrupting Jillian's train of thought. *We must plan our escape from the castle. We must also find a way to free the magical creatures that are trapped here. You see, I have been observing the castle for some time now. About two years ago it became evident that a number of magical creatures were disappearing from all over North of North. I began investigating and eventually traced the missing animals to Styginmoor.*

"So you were looking for the creatures that day when I saw you outside the castle grounds?" asked Jillian.

That's right. It was very foolish of me to let myself be seen like that. Although I do not regret that it has led me to you, the otter replied.

"I still don't understand," said Jillian. "Does Ivenna know I have the ability to summon animals? Has she been using me to draw magical creatures to Styginmoor? She already has plenty of servants. Why should she want more?"

Yes, she knows about your ability. I suspect she is collecting the animals so she can steal their magic and use it to increase her own, answered the otter. *For many years Ivenna has searched for a way to overcome her sworn enemies, the Valkyries. They are the first horse riders. My good friend is the leader of all horses, Bella.*

At once, Jillian pictured the white horse she had seen in her daydream.

"Bella," she whispered. Saying the name aloud sent a tingle across her skin.

Before Jillian could ask any more questions, she heard a rustling at the door. The otter's eyes went wide with fear.

Someone was listening.

Jillian whipped around. There in the doorway was the hulking frame of a wolf.

CHAPTER 3

For a moment Jillian went ice-cold. Then she recognized the wolf.

"Conall!" she cried. "You scared me half to death!"

The big wolf huffed softly, the sound almost like a snorting chuckle.

"Don't worry," Jillian explained to the otter. "This is Conall. He's not like the other wolves."

Conall growled.

"Well, you're *not*," Jillian insisted. "Even if you are looking more and more like Myrfor every day. No one could call you the runt of the litter anymore, could they, Fuzzy Foot?"

Jillian and Conall had grown up together in the castle. Smaller than his littermates, Conall's sweet nature had endeared him to Jillian from the first. Even though Ivenna and Myrfor had tried to keep them apart, the girl and the wolf shared a brother-and-sister-like bond. Some days they were the best of friends. Other days they got under each other's skin in ways no one else could.

The other thing that set Conall apart from the rest of the wolves was his silence. Although he barked and growled like any wolf, he had never once spoken the wolf language. Myrfor and Ivenna thought he was mute. Jillian wondered if it had more to do with his goodness. The wolf tongue just sounded *evil*. No one could use it to say kindly things.

As they'd gotten older, Conall had grown large and strong. He was one of the biggest wolves now, nearly as massive as his father, Myrfor. He was the swiftest runner and the stealthiest stalker in the pack. In spite of the fact that he didn't talk, Ivenna and Myrfor were starting to notice him. The wolves were beginning to whisper that Conall was the most likely successor to Myrfor.

Although she still believed in Conall's goodness, Jillian had begun to feel a distance growing between herself and her friend. She feared that the day was coming when Conall would be forced to choose between the wolves and his friendship with her. She wished she could be sure of how he would choose.

Conall's sudden appearance here in the otter's room was no accident. Jillian knew she was taking too long with the key. Ivenna and Myrfor must have sent Conall to track her down, maybe even to spy. They, too, had their doubts about his loyalty and tested him whenever they could.

Jillian turned to the otter. "I'm sorry," she said. "I have to leave you here for now. But I promise I'll come back as soon as possible."

The otter nodded. Conall grunted impatiently.

"All right, Fuzzy Foot," Jillian said. "Let's go."

When they reached the dining room, Ivenna and Myrfor were waiting.

"Good work, Conall," Ivenna said. "You are dismissed."

Conall slinked away without looking back.

Jillian approached Ivenna, holding out the key.

"What took you so long, girl?" Ivenna snapped, snatching the key from Jillian's grasp. "Learning about our new guest, were you? Anything you want to share?"

"No. I simply did as you told me and delivered the porridge," Jillian said, as calmly as possible. She couldn't let

Ivenna know her mind was racing with thoughts of the otter, the great horse Bella, and everything she had just learned about her own powers.

Myrfor sniffed and sucked at a scrap of meat in his teeth. "The girl is a liar," he snarled. "I can smell the lies."

"Yes, yes," Ivenna said. "I don't believe she's telling the whole truth either. But I do trust she'd let us know if she'd learned anything upsetting. She simply couldn't hide it. She *is* such a delicate soul when it comes to magical creatures."

Ivenna looked at Jillian. It was a test to see if her words had hit their mark, to find out what she knew. But Jillian kept cool, giving away nothing.

"Is that all, mistress?" she asked.

Ivenna's eyes narrowed. "This conversation is finished . . . for tonight," she said. "Now go and see to my bath."

Jillian walked swiftly from the dining room, but paused outside the door to listen. She heard Ivenna cross the room to Myrfor.

"Guard this closely," Ivenna said. "The girl was obviously hiding something. I don't know what it was, but she must never again be alone in the room with the otter."

Jillian stumbled to Ivenna's bathing chamber. She felt as if she were walking through swamp fog. Her head was swimming with all she had learned.

In the bathing room, bubble turtles were already toiling away, creating mountains of lather. Tassel mice stood at attention, ready for their hair brushing and braiding duties.

It's my fault they're all trapped here, forced to work long into the night, Jillian thought sadly.

Ivenna had used her to draw the creatures to Styginmoor Castle and a life of servitude. Who knew what else she had in store for them?

A cloud of guilt settled on Jillian's

chest until she felt she could barely breathe.

I can't let this go on. I have to do something, she said to herself.

Rushing back to her small room, Jillian ran over to the loose stone in the wall. She would get her journal and make the drawing of the great white horse, Bella. If Jillian could summon other creatures by drawing them in her memory journal, she was sure she could summon Bella, too. The leader of all horses would help the otter and the other magical creatures in the castle. Wouldn't she? *But what if Bella got caught in Ivenna's grasp, too?* Jillian wondered. *Then we'd all be in danger.* Then Jillian remembered her dream of Bella and the magic that emanated from her white coat and gold-flecked eyes. A horse that spectacular would find a way to evade Ivenna's cruel tricks.

Jillian's heart raced as she slid the stone aside and reached into the nook.

Her hand felt around the dark space for the journal. She reached and reached.

There was nothing there. The journal was gone.

*J*illian woke the next day at sunrise. It was a new day, and she had to make a new plan. She wouldn't rest until the otter and the other magical creatures were free—and that meant she had to find a way to summon Bella.

As Jillian gazed out her tiny window, the fog-shrouded landscape seemed almost beautiful. She felt a sense of power and purpose, as if a light had gone on inside her and nothing could put it out.

After attending to the breakfast duties, Jillian went down to the laundry in the basement of the castle. The room was warm, the air thick with steam. Laundry bubbled away in massive cauldrons heated by fire spoops. Whiffle bears flew this way and that, sprinkling lavender and rose petals into the wash water.

It crushed Jillian to think of these gentle creatures working long hours every day to serve a mistress as cold and ungrateful as Ivenna.

"How can I help?" Jillian asked her friends. She was always happy to pitch in, but her mind also swirled with the plan she was making. And the first part of her plan was finding an excuse to slip outside to find Conall.

Jillian spied a large basket of wet laundry sitting on one of the work tables. "I'll hang these linens out in the fresh air," she said.

Jillian lugged the heavy basket up many flights of stone stairs and outside to the castle grounds. As she stepped outdoors, she blinked. It took a moment for her eyes to adjust. When they did, she caught her breath. Sunlight! Actual sunlight!

The sun hardly ever appeared around Styginmoor Castle, and Jillian was unaccustomed to it. But today the usual fog was swirling, shredding, as shafts of light from the sky pierced the gloom. There were even small patches of blue here and there. Although winter wasn't quite over yet, the air had a tinge of warmth in it—as if the weather itself had decided to cooperate with her plans.

Glancing around, Jillian found two trees she could use to string up a clothesline. She placed the basket on the ground and set to work.

As Jillian finished tying the line, she heard ferocious snarling behind her. A pack of young wolves snapped and growled at each other as their game of hunt-and-catch spilled across the lawn to where Jillian was working. She knew the wolves were just playing, but the violence of their game made her shudder.

A particularly large wolf came bounding after the others. *Conall.*

Jillian had to get his attention. She needed her friend to help with her plan.

The pack began to move past Jillian as Conall closed in on them.

"Pssst! Fuzzy Foot!" Jillian whispered from behind a wet sheet. "Over here."

Conall's ears twitched, and his head whipped around. He froze mid-stride, breaking off his chase. After looking around cautiously, he approached Jillian. She felt his hesitation.

"Sorry to interrupt your game," Jillian said. "But I need your help. I've got to see the otter again. It's the only way to help the magical creatures. That means I have to get the key from Myrfor. I was thinking, since you're a wolf, it would be easier for you to . . ."

Conall gave Jillian a look that stopped her mid-sentence.

"I know it's not easy for you, Fuzzy Foot," Jillian said. Her heart ached for him, torn as he was between his tribe and his own kind heart. "I know you're one of them. But you're *different*, too."

The breeze shifted. Jillian looked up and saw Myrfor across the grounds. On a day like this, he was likely coming to round up the young wolves for a hunt in the woods.

Conall had also noticed him. Giving Jillian one last glance, he turned and ran to catch up with the pack. Jillian's heart sank.

She knew Conall had to do what the other wolves expected of him. Going against them would be too difficult. Still, she was hurt. Jillian used to think he would be on her side forever. Now she wasn't so sure.

She took a deep breath. She was going to have to find a way to get the key from Myrfor herself.

Myrfor was too strong for Jillian

to confront directly. She would never win in a battle against him. The only way she was going to get the key was if she could find a way to sneak up on him.

Maybe I can steal the key while he sleeps tonight, thought Jillian. She shook her head impatiently. *No, that's impossible. Everyone knows he sleeps lightly and wakes at even the smallest noise.*

Unless . . .

Suddenly Jillian knew exactly what to do.

With many of the wolves away on their hunt and Ivenna within the castle walls, Jillian had the perfect chance to carry out her new plan.

First, she had to sneak into to the castle herbarium.

Unless she was given orders to fetch something for Ivenna, Jillian was strictly forbidden from going to the herbarium. She would have to be very careful.

Jillian kept the laundry basket and one wet sheet with her in case she ran into anyone. If she were caught, she could pretend she was just going out to put the sheet on the line.

Across the back field, a few rose dragons tended an outdoor garden. Everything was quiet and still as Jillian approached the herbarium. She always felt this was a magical place, with its shiny rows of colored glass jars, its exotic hothouse plants, and its deep spicy scent.

Peering through a large glass window, Jillian saw no one inside the herbarium. So far, so good. On such a day, she knew the master herbalist was likely to go out gathering herbs with the tea leaf pandas and ivy-tailed dragons. These creatures knew how to find plants and roots better than any other.

In the right hands, potions made from roots and herbs could be used to do wonderful things—heal wounds, mend broken wings, cure sickness. But in the dark world of Wolf Riders like Ivenna, potions were used for far more selfish purposes—learning secrets, making threats, and using dark magic.

As Jillian thought of Ivenna, her resolve was renewed. She carefully cracked open the herbarium door. The smell of plants and potions drifted over her.

"Now," Jillian whispered to herself, "I just have to find the right herbs."

She stared up at a wall of glass jars. There were hundreds of them, carefully arranged by color and name, containing every type of herb and root imaginable.

"*Arrowroot . . . baneberry . . . bearsfoot . . . belladonna . . .*"

Bella. Jillian thought of the great white horse. Her pulse quickened as she moved to the next row of jars with new determination.

But after several minutes and many more rows, she grew frustrated. There were too many jars, and she didn't know the first thing about plants. She had been hoping to find the master herbalist's book of recipes, but he must have either hidden it or taken it with him.

"*Salvia . . . sansevieria . . .* It's no use!" she cried. "I'll never find the right herb for a sleeping potion."

Jillian's eyes welled up with tears. What was she going to do?

Crash! Something hit the floor behind her and shattered. Jillian ducked for cover behind a large wooden collection chest. Her heart beat wildly. Had she been caught?

Seconds ticked by and no one hauled her out from her hiding place. Finally, Jillian summoned the courage to peek out.

When she did, she saw a gorgeous violet pixie hovering in the air, its shiny purple wings glinting in the light. A blue glass jar lay smashed on the flagstones. Dried leaves were scattered everywhere.

"Is this . . . what I'm looking for?" Jillian stammered.

The violet pixie swooped down and circled the broken glass jar, and then flew off through the open door.

"Thank you," Jillian whispered. Maybe she wasn't alone after all.

Jillian plucked the herbs from the floor and then carefully swept up the broken glass. She couldn't risk the master herbalist finding it and becoming suspicious.

Jillian tucked both glass and herbs into the laundry basket and draped the wet sheet over the top. Her plan was under way.

5

"Thank you, friend," Jillian said, taking a fresh bunch of sorrel from a bobolink. Jillian chopped the herbs and sprinkled them over Ivenna's and Myrfor's dinners. They were having Ivenna's favorite dish, turtle soup.

Little did Ivenna know that Jillian's recipe lacked one crucial ingredient—turtle. Jillian had secretly changed the recipe long ago, so that no creatures would be harmed. Instead of turtle, the soup was filled with big chunks of meaty mushrooms. And tonight the soup would contain something extra special—the herbs from the herbarium.

The pipsqueak longtails who were in charge of the dining room came scurrying through the kitchen, ready to set the table and prepare for service. Ivenna and Myrfor would be there in minutes.

Jillian's heart pounded. An anxious knot formed in her chest. What if the herbs didn't work? If the plan went wrong, she and the others would be in great danger. Jillian didn't even want to think about what Ivenna might do to them all if she even suspected what Jillian was up to.

She told herself to stop fretting. It would do no good. "There is no other way," she reminded herself.

From the hallway, she heard the click of Ivenna's staff tapping on the stone floor. *This is it*, she thought.

For better or worse, there was no going back now.

* * *

"If there's one thing that stupid girl does know how to do, it's make turtle soup," Ivenna remarked, reaching for her spoon.

Across the table, Myrfor salivated at the smells wafting from his bowl.

"I hope you like it," Jillian said. "I made extra so that you could each have two servings." She forced a smile and curtseyed before leaving the room.

After Ivenna and Myrfor had finished their second helpings of soup, Jillian returned to clear the dishes. Entering the dining room, she was greeted with the sounds of snoring. Ivenna's snore was a shrill whistle; Myrfor's was a deep rumble.

The herbs had worked!

Jillian had to act fast. She didn't know how long Ivenna and Myrfor would be asleep. If they woke while she was gone, they would realize something was wrong and sound the alarm.

Her hands shaking, Jillian quietly

approached Myrfor. His massive frame shook with each grumbling snore. Jillian hesitated. Even asleep, the great black wolf was terrifying.

"Don't be a baby," she whispered to herself. "You brought the magical creatures here. It's up to you to free them."

Jillian grasped the chain around Myrfor's neck and lifted it up carefully. It caught momentarily in his thick black fur, but she pulled it free, sliding it over his big, pointed ears.

She raced through the castle to the secret wing where the otter was being held prisoner. Reaching the wooden door, she quickly turned the key in the lock and pushed it open.

"I'm back," Jillian cried, gasping for breath.

The otter turned calmly, as if expecting her.

"I . . . I don't know how long I have, or even what I'm supposed to do,"

Jillian said. "I just knew I had to get back here."

Approaching Jillian, the otter bent her elegant neck and gestured to the stone around her neck.

The Starstone.

"The Starstone." Jillian echoed. The stone glowed brightly, and she reached out to touch it.

Take it. You or your messenger will need it.

Gently, Jillian lifted the necklace from the otter's delicate neck and placed it on her own. Immediately, her senses tingled and her mind sharpened. Staring into the otter's eyes, she felt the connection between them. The stone really did allow the wearer to see what others nearby were thinking.

The otter nodded intently.

Get to Bella at Trails End and ask her for help. She will know what to do. Be brave, little one. Many depend on you, and you are stronger than you think.

No sooner had the otter's message filled Jillian's mind than a sharp pain seared her.

Wolves! The pack was stirring. Had someone raised the alarm?

With the Starstone in her possession, Jillian could feel the wolves' energy, like a dark and dangerous storm cloud coming toward her.

Before Jillian could act, Conall burst into the room.

"Conall!" Jillian cried. "How did you know where to find me?"

Conall ignored her question. His eyes were hard and bright as he scanned the room anxiously. His whole body seemed tense and alert.

"What is it?" she demanded. "What's wrong?"

His thoughts came pouring directly into her mind. It was the first time he had ever communicated directly with her. But there was no time to marvel.

Some wolf guards found Myrfor asleep and were unable to rouse him. They don't know what is happening, but they are in a frenzy. You have put yourself and others in great danger.

"It was the only way," Jillian cried. "I have to free the otter and the magical creatures. You know Ivenna is holding them here against their will. Even worse than that, I think she's trying to steal their magic for her own evil purposes. She must be stopped. Please, Conall, you know what I'm saying is true. Do what's right."

The howls of the wolf pack grew nearer.

Jillian looked deep into her friend's eyes. "We have no time. We must get to the horse Bella at Trails End. She is the leader of the Great Herd. She will know what to do. *You* must do it, Conall. You're a wolf. You can slip away without being noticed. I'll never make it out of here."

Conall's response came at once,

his fear and anger raging.

You ask too much. Trails End is the heart of the enemy's empire. No wolf could possibly enter such a place.

"Conall, your heart is good," Jillian cried. "You're not like the others. If you won't listen to me, listen to your heart."

Suddenly, a screech echoed through the hallway. "Get the girl!"

It was Ivenna! The herbs had worn off. She and Myrfor had woken.

Jillian gazed at Conall, her eyes begging. "Please . . . Fuzzy Foot. Please! There's no other way!"

Conall stared back at Jillian. Years ago she had befriended him, the unwanted runt of the litter. Now he was a large wolf, second only to Myrfor. She was still a little wisp of a girl, thin as a wood sprite, but braver and truer than any wolf he knew.

Conall bared his teeth. *Give me the Starstone.*

Jillian slipped the stone around Conall's neck. "Thank you," she whispered.

Moments later, the wolf pack burst through the door. Myrfor led the way. Snarling and growling, the wolves began to circle Jillian.

In the chaos, Conall slipped away.

Hidden in a dark nook in the hallway, Conall glanced back at his friend. His heart burned with anger as he saw her small frame disappear behind Myrfor's hulking shadow. The Starstone glowed softly. Wearing it, Conall could see clearly the dark depths of Myrfor's evil soul.

Fearing Myrfor's wrath, Conall had tried all his life to fit in with the pack. He got no pleasure from mindless hunting, but had worked hard to become a fearless predator. Over time, his skill and strength had grown until no one but Myrfor could best him. He was Myrfor's son, and it was increasingly accepted that one day he would lead the pack.

But now, seeing into Myrfor's black soul, Conall knew that day would never come. He needed to be true to himself.

More than anything, Conall wished he could go back and save Jillian, but he knew he must do what she had asked of him, no matter what. It was up to him to go to Trails End and find the great horse Bella.

Not knowing what danger he might face, Conall raced into the night.

*I*cy wind rushed through Conall's fur as he ran deep into the forest.

Styginmoor Castle grew smaller and smaller, until it was just an eerily glowing spot in the landscape, miles away. Conall's heart pounded. The Starstone thudded against his chest. He didn't dare stop. The others might soon discover him missing and be on his trail.

His spirit shrank from the thought of what he must do now. Trails End was many days' journey from here, and he wasn't even entirely sure which direction to go. But he had to get there—now!—and find this horse, Bella. If he didn't, Jillian and the others might be lost forever.

There was only one way to get there fast enough.

The Shadow Path.

The Shadow Path was a magical road that could be traveled only by wolves and their riders. It allowed its users to cheat time and traverse the world in a single night.

Like all young wolves, Conall had grown up hearing tales of the mysterious path from Myrfor and the elders. The Shadow Path was twisted and dangerous. Only the bravest and strongest could withstand its dark magic. Many wolves had entered it, never to return.

The way to find the Shadow Path, Conall knew, was to allow *it* to find *you*. So, running headlong into the night, Conall closed his eyes and let the darkness envelop him.

Suddenly, a powerful force gripped him. He was sucked through a whirlpool of crushing energy. His muscles tensed and the roots of his fur tingled. He didn't fight, and instead allowed himself to be whisked away.

A sound began throbbing in Conall's ears. It grew louder, until it thundered like an enormous waterfall.

Then, in an instant, all fell silent. The ground was no longer beneath Conall's feet. He was surrounded by nothingness.

A feeling of empty isolation filled him. He had entered the Shadow Path.

Conall knew enough about the path to keep his eyes clenched firmly shut. To open them meant exposure to the darkest evil—and certain doom. No wolf had ever opened his eyes on the Shadow Path and lived to tell the tale.

So Conall ran blindly onward, straining his muscles against the empty

air. As he ventured farther along the path, his fierce hunter's instincts sharpened. Strange sounds and smells swirled all around him. Something was coming, but *what?* And *when?*

The first icy blast made Conall shudder. A moment afterward, what felt like dozens of bony fingers began scrabbling at his fur, probing deep under his skin, piercing into his very heart. Voices whined around him—or was it the wind itself? *Conall . . . Conall . . . we are hungry . . . feed us, Conall . . . give us your warmth, we are so cold . . . Conall . . .*

The worst thing was, he *recognized* some of the voices. The urge to open his eyes and see who was speaking was almost harder to bear than the pain.

Fighting against both the urge and the pain, he pushed on.

The longer he traveled, the more the phantoms tugged at him. Shadows and spirits surrounded him, trying to pull him off the Shadow Path and into the Shadow Realm itself. He understood now that these were lost souls that had once traveled the path, but had not made it out.

With each step Conall took, he felt more energy drain from his body. His limbs became lead weights, and he felt an overwhelming urge to stop, lie down, and sleep. He knew, though, that if he stopped, it would be forever.

Keep moving, he told himself. *Just keep moving. Never stop.*

Conall's mind wandered to its darkest corners. An image of Myrfor, fangs bared, cornering a helpless Jillian flashed through his head. In his gut he felt the hatred of the wolf pack, which could so quickly turn on one of its own. Then he saw Ivenna smiling cruelly as she raised her staff high to strike Jillian down.

The images piled on one after another like stones in the castle wall, until Conall thought his mind and heart would burst from their weight.

Then, just as he felt he could take no more, the probing of the icy fingers stopped. The voices cut off suddenly, as if a door had closed. The dark thoughts lifted.

The air grew warmer, denser. And the ground! Once again, it was firm beneath his tired feet!

Conall felt his lungs expand as fear and pain drained from him. He had made it through the Shadow Path.

Unless the feeling of safety was just one more trick . . .

Only one way to find out. His heart pounding wildly, Conall opened his eyes.

7

*B*linking against the breaking light of dawn, Conall slowly glanced around. He stood high on a rocky ledge overlooking a landscape like none he had ever imagined.

In the distance, trees seemed to burst with lush green leaves. A waterfall cascaded crystal-blue water that sparkled like sapphires. Instead of a sinister stone castle, there were dozens of small, thatched farm cottages surrounding a little town. Farther out, wisps of fog rose from a broad river that flowed into a huge body of water. Conall had never seen the ocean before, but water that wide could be nothing else.

Conall breathed in so deeply, he almost choked. The air was crisp and pure.

So this was Trails End, home of his supposed enemies.

Used to the dark world of Styginmoor Castle, Conall felt like a stranger amid such brightness. What was a wolf like him doing in a place like this?

He shook himself briskly, brushing aside his doubt. He was on a mission. He had to find the leader of the magical horses, Bella.

Boldly, Conall leaped down the side of the hill and trotted straight into the heart of the town.

"A wolf!" someone cried.

A flurry of gasps and whispers rippled through the streets. Horses scattered and people shuttered their windows. Others hurried children indoors.

A brave group of humans and horses remained to face down their enemy.

"Why have you come here?" a man shouted at Conall.

"Look," another gasped, pointing. "The wolf wears a Starstone."

Murmurs erupted from the group.

The stone pulsed around Conall's neck. Using its power, he sent his thought out. *I seek the great horse Bella.*

"Bella! The wolf wants to see Bella!" More murmurs. Conall could read the humans' fear and confusion clearly.

"We can't take him to Bella," said an old woman. "We don't know if he can be trusted, even if he does have a Starstone. He could have taken it by force."

The group began to argue among themselves in low tones.

Conall grew frustrated. He had come too far to be stopped by a group of foolish humans and horses. What did they know?

Then, abruptly, the group ceased its whispering. A hush fell.

At the same time, Conall felt his mind relax. Sensing a presence behind him, he turned.

There stood a majestic white horse. She was surrounded by a soft, white aura that shimmered like stardust. The horse looked at Conall. Her dark eyes glowed with a warm, penetrating energy.

I am Bella. What is your name, wolf?

Conall gazed back, trying to conceal his awe.

I am Conall, son of Myrfor, scion of Fenrir.

Conall's pedigree gave him great standing among the wolf pack. He was descended from the boldest and most legendary of wolves. But now, as the great horse looked down at him, Conall felt only shame.

You are bred of wicked stock. You are the son of death and destruction. Why do you appear before me?

Conall thought about the otter and all the magical creatures held captive at Styginmoor Castle. Then he thought about Jillian and remembered her words, *You are not like the other wolves.*

Bella nodded at him. She saw Conall's mind and the reason for his journey. Conall suspected she would have known, even had he not had the Starstone.

You may yet prove better than your ancestors. I will help you, but we must hurry. Quickly, follow me.

The great white horse began to gallop away, and Conall fell into step behind her. Before he realized what was happening, Conall gazed down to see the ground disappearing below him. Together they had risen in the air and were running on the wind.

Conall glanced nervously at Bella.

Her gold-flecked gaze steadied him.

Don't be afraid. You are with me. And soon the others will come.

Others? Conall asked.

Yes. We will need help if we are to save your friend Jillian and the great Starstone Otter Queen, as well as the other magical creatures.

Stars emerged from Bella's glowing white aura, flying off through the sky in four directions. She and Conall went higher and higher, Bella leading the way into the heavens.

Moments later, the sky crackled with a bright white light. Conall recoiled, almost losing his pace. There was a loud clap of thunder, and a massive black stallion appeared.

Emerging from the clouds with swift strides, he quickly caught up to Bella. The stallion glanced at her, and then at Conall. A snort escaped his nostrils.

What is this wolf doing here?

Never slowing, Bella eyed the stallion at her side.

He is our ally, Thunder. I will explain soon. There is little time now.

Bella drove harder into the wind, the great black stallion racing alongside her at the speed of lightning. Conall struggled to keep up with the two powerful creatures, but he was determined and pushed himself onward.

Soon a third magnificent horse appeared, carried along the wind by an enormous pair of shimmering wings. Her sleek coat was a soft brown, and she was draped in silken ribbons.

Nike. Bella nodded to greet her.

Then two more great horses appeared. Fiona, a fiery red filly, and Jewel, a mahogany bay mare whose eyes sparkled as brightly as the gems that dotted her forehead and dark mane.

Each of the horses had answered Bella's call without question, but Conall could feel their sharp suspicion of him.

Wolves and Wolf Riders were the sworn enemies of horses.

The Starstone conveyed the horses' distrust and doubt to Conall.

Nike, the winged horse, looked to Bella.

What are we to do with this wolf who nips at our heels?

Bella's answer projected back, clear and strong.

He is here with my blessing. You must trust me.

Thunder glared at Conall.

If he so much as snarls in my direction, I'll strike him down with the fury of the North Wind.

Conall felt shunned, much as he had as the runt of his litter years ago. Bella looked sternly at the black horse.

Calm yourself, Thunder. Save your wrath for those who deserve it. This wolf is not our enemy, but we shall soon face many who are.

* * *

Traveling the sky with Bella and the others, Conall eventually began to feel a deep sense of peace.

Maybe Jillian was right. Maybe he *was* different from the other wolves. As he had this thought, Bella glanced back and gave him a knowing nod.

But suddenly another feeling overtook Conall. Looking ahead, he saw a patch of dark gray clouds. A sense of doom swelled up within him, as it had on the Shadow Path.

The horses began to slow their pace. Conall caught up to Bella. He was filled with fear.

What is that . . . place?

Bella gazed back, a glimmer of sadness in her remarkable eyes.

Why, Conall, don't you recognize Styginmoor Castle?

CHAPTER

8

As he stood outside the castle walls, Conall felt as if he were seeing Styginmoor for the first time. A cold shiver ran through him as he gazed at the menacing black castle, its stone turrets rising high into the dark sky boiling with storm clouds. There was no light here, nothing pure or good. Had he really called this place his home?

Bella and the other horses prepared for the attack. The horses were brave and powerful creatures, but taking the castle would be extremely dangerous.

The group was greatly outnumbered. And Conall knew better than any creature just how fierce the wolf pack could be. Myrfor was merciless and demanded the same from the other wolves.

Still, there was no time to lose. They had to act quickly to save Jillian and the others.

Bella's white mane glowed brightly against dark gray clouds. She looked at Conall, her eyes filled with determination.

When we enter the castle, I want you to find Jillian and the Starstone Otter Queen. It's up to you to see that they are safe. Stop at nothing.

Conall nodded bravely, although his heart began to beat more quickly.

Thunder, go now!

Thunder, the great black horse, stomped and reared. Bolts of lightning exploded from his hooves, slamming into the castle gates. They cracked and split like twigs before an ax, falling into a pile of dust and kindling.

Conall heard a deep, low howl resounding through the castle walls. He knew the sound deep in his bones. Myrfor was mobilizing the wolves. In a moment they would be flooding out in formation—fierce and ready to fight.

The time had come.

Thunder pounded ahead, leading the rest of the group through the fallen gates. Nike, the majestic winged horse, streaked up into the sky. Hovering above the castle, she scanned the dark maze of corridors below for captive animals in need of rescue, occasionally dipping and diving for a closer look.

Suddenly, Myrfor emerged from a doorway into the courtyard, hulking and ferocious. His eyes glowed with evil excitement, and his fur stood on end. Behind him were seemingly endless rows of snarling, snapping wolves. They faced the horses. Myrfor threw back his head and howled.

Conall raced toward the castle, hugging the shadows so he wouldn't be noticed. He couldn't risk the wolves or Ivenna seeing him with the Starstone. If they learned Conall was against them, he would never be able to save Jillian. He would have to do his best to blend in. In the chaos of battle, he just might be able to get away with it.

Conall felt guilty, once again pretending to be something he was not. But he would do whatever it took to find Jillian and the Starstone Otter Queen.

As Conall moved through the shadows, he saw Nike dive from the air, swooping low to the ground to distract a group of wolves. They leaped up, snapping at her hooves. Fluttering in the air just out of their reach, she kicked and bucked.

Jewel, the stately bay, seized the moment and raced into the castle to search out the magical creatures. Once released, they could join the horses in battle.

The wolves attacking Nike were becoming frenzied. One of them scrambled onto its fellows' backs and leaped up, snapping at Nike's flank. The chestnut mare neighed in pain. Then she gave a powerful thrust of her wings and shot skyward. The wolves were left writhing in a heap below.

Wolves continued filing out of the castle halls in endless legions. Myrfor's deep barking growls directed their moves. Conall could see that, in no time, the horses would be surrounded.

Where was Bella? Conall realized suddenly that he hadn't seen the great white mare since Thunder broke down the gates. He paused, dread suddenly turning his limbs to jelly.

As Thunder whirled and stomped at the wolves around him, Fiona, the fiery red horse, broke away. Racing in circles around the courtyard, her mane became a blur and her vibrant coat began to glow. Her hooves flashed and a blazing trail of fire erupted from behind her.

Wolves howled as the flames lapped nearer, trapping them outside the fiery ring and blinding their vision with smoke and white-hot flame. Several retreated in fear, fleeing past Conall. Then the fiery ring smoldered down, and the smoke began to drift off in wisps through the sky.

There in the center of it all stood Bella.

Calm and majestic, the beautiful white horse was not daunted by the slavering, growling wolves. She walked through the middle of the courtyard slowly, seeming to take no notice of them as they circled in from all sides.

When the wolves were just inches away from her, Bella reared up and tossed her stately head. Her bright neigh, like the sound of a thousand crystal bells, echoed off the walls of the courtyard. The wolves all around her stopped in their tracks, sensing the strange and unusual power that filled the air.

Conall saw a flash of pure white light, so bright he had to close his eyes for fear of being blinded. When he looked back, the wolves around Bella had transformed from huge, menacing creatures to small cubs tumbling on the ground.

Conall couldn't help but be amused at the once-black-hearted beasts now nipping playfully at one another's tails.

Maybe there's hope for them after all, he thought, as he slipped into the castle. He made his way down pitch-black corridors until he came to a great wooden door near Ivenna's chambers.

Conall felt the Starstone around his neck glowing, and he felt confident. Someone or *something* was inside. He was sure.

He threw his weight against the solid door, and it slowly opened. . . .

There, trapped in a large iron cage, was the Starstone Otter Queen.

The otter's bright eyes locked on Conall's, the Starstone connecting their minds.

You were true to your word. You returned.

Conall was heartened by the otter's kind thought, but his heart plunged. Where was Jillian? It had never occurred to him she and the otter wouldn't be together.

The otter gazed at him gently.

You will find your friend. I am quite sure she is close by.

Conall wasted no time. He set to work freeing the otter, chewing through the thick leather straps that secured the cage door. At last, the cage swung open and the otter stepped out delicately.

Take the stone, Conall said, bowing his head toward the otter so she could lift it from his neck. *I no longer need it. Go to the courtyard where your friend Bella awaits your help. There are others to be saved.*

With that, the great wolf turned and sped off through the corridor. Jillian was somewhere within these dark, stone walls. He would find her.

9

"Don't make me ask again," Ivenna hissed. "Who helped you summon *her* here?"

Jillian knew at once Ivenna was speaking of Bella. Conall must have been successful on his journey. Now, he and Bella had returned to the castle.

Jillian sat, captive in Ivenna's private chambers, staring back in silence. She would never tell that Conall had helped her.

"You really are a foolish child, with your little dreams and *doodles*." Ivenna's tone softened slightly, and an evil smile danced across her lips. "I had such high hopes for you, all those years ago."

Jillian's mind raced. *Play dumb. Don't give anything away. Let her think she has the upper hand.*

"Yes, my darling," Ivenna continued. "I know all about your little drawings—all those memories, all those creatures. I've been looking at your journal for years. How else would I know which of your little friends to expect at the castle—how best to capture them and use them to serve me? Oh, don't worry, your precious book is perfectly safe. In fact, here it is."

Ivenna pulled the small midnight-blue leather journal from her cloak and threw it on the ground in front of Jillian. The book landed with a thud, tumbling open to the page with the drawing of the otter. Jillian's heart tightened in her chest.

"I'm curious," Ivenna purred. As

the Wolf Rider gazed at her, Jillian felt uncomfortably like a mouse in the gaze of a hungry cat. "Did you *really* believe your precious journal came from that ragtag gypsy family of yours? As if *they* could give you something so magical and marvelous. They could barely put clothes on your back."

A lump grew in Jillian's throat. She felt her eyes well up with tears. *Her family.* All these years, she had yearned for some connection—some memory, some dream of them.

"Stop!" Jillian cried. "Don't you dare speak of them!"

"Still pining for the past, are you?" Ivenna said. "You should be grateful that I rescued you from that bunch of worthless fools. I had heard of your ability to communicate with animals. People said that, even as a baby, wherever you went, magical creatures would follow. But your family didn't know what to do with you. They would never have appreciated your special talents the way I have. You see, I had the magical journal and quill, but they wouldn't work for me. No, the magic required someone pure of heart, someone who was open to the goodness in magical creatures. Someone like you. I did you a favor by taking you from those worthless gypsies."

Jillian gasped. The painful truth washed over her.

Her family had not abandoned her as Ivenna had always said. Instead, Ivenna had stolen her away from them and used her to call magical creatures to the castle. Images of the happy life she could have had flashed through her mind.

Jillian's heart was breaking for all that she had lost. But as strong as that feeling was the fierce new resolve that burned inside her. She glared at Ivenna, defiant. Ivenna had stolen her from her family, but she would steal no more.

Just then, a howl tore through the walls of the castle, shaking its very stones.

Ivenna jerked her head around. Her eyes narrowed.

"That's Myrfor," she whispered. "The battle has begun."

Whipping her head back, the Wolf Rider stared at Jillian. Her eyes blazed with fury. She pointed a bony finger toward the blank page in the notebook. "If you didn't use your notebook to summon that . . . that creature, then someone else must have brought her here. I will find out who, and you will both pay."

Ivenna grabbed Jillian roughly by the arm. "Now, come with me!"

Jillian reached down to snatch the notebook as she rose. But when her fingers made contact with the soft worn leather, she felt Ivenna's nails dig into the flesh of her arm.

"I'll be taking that," Ivenna said.

Reluctantly, Jillian surrendered the journal.

Ivenna thrust the book back in the folds of her cloak, yanking Jillian toward the door of the chamber with her other hand.

"Let go of me," Jillian protested, trying to pull free from Ivenna's grasp.

"There's no use fighting, you stupid child," Ivenna said. "I'm going to put you somewhere you won't be found. Then, I am going to defend my castle against unwelcome guests."

Jillian glared at Ivenna. Ivenna gave her a cruel smile.

"Oh, don't worry, child, you won't miss out on the action. You'll have a perfect view of Myrfor and me destroying your new friend, Bella."

Jillian stood helplessly, gazing out the turret windows at the courtyard below. It was complete chaos. Wolves and wolf cubs ran this way and that, snarling and growling.

Two magnificent horses—a large black stallion and a blazing red mare—lunged at the wolves from two sides, corralling them in one section of the courtyard.

"Oh, the horses," Jillian whispered. "They're so beautiful."

Another horse appeared. A rich reddish brown, with a dark mane and glowing gems studding its muzzle, it was just as beautiful as the other two.

Aboard the red-brown horse were magical creatures of all kinds—bubble turtles, pipsqueak longtails, tassel mice. Jillian could scarcely believe her eyes.

Her magical friends were being rescued!

Jillian searched the crowd for Conall.

"Fuzzy Foot, where are you?" she murmured.

Just then, a huge black wolf appeared below her. He stalked to the center of the courtyard, teeth bared, snarling. Myrfor!

He let out a deep, angry growl. A challenge.

Myrfor's opponent came into view, a majestic white horse surrounded by a cloud of softly glowing light.

Jillian gasped. *"Bella!"*

Here was the mysterious horse from her visions—right before her very eyes!

Myrfor howled and attacked. Jillian's heart pounded. She could barely watch.

Bella evaded Myrfor's malicious lunges, showing no fear. Again and again Myrfor was repelled, as if the white light around the great mare could not be penetrated.

Then Ivenna swept into the courtyard behind Myrfor, her cape billowing, a black trail in her wake. The weak daylight seemed to dim even further as she raised her metal staff. Even from high above, Jillian could sense the rage coming from her mistress.

Suddenly, a beam of brilliant light shot forth from the gloom. It hit Ivenna

and she stumbled, blinded by the light.

There, across the courtyard, stood the Starstone Otter Queen, sending a white-hot beam at Ivenna from the blue stone around her neck. Jillian's heart leaped. The beautiful creature she had befriended was free from her stone prison.

The black stallion stomped at the ground and sent a shock of lightning toward the disoriented Ivenna. The lightning bolt hit Ivenna's staff, sending bolts of electricity through Ivenna's body. Ivenna dropped her staff and collapsed onto the ground in a daze.

The red mare, joined quickly by the black stallion, kept the other wolves at bay, while the brown horse shuttled the last of the magical creatures to safety beyond the courtyard walls.

The Starstone Otter Queen scurried to Bella and leaped onto her back. Bella galloped swiftly across the courtyard. Poised on Bella's back, the otter looked even more regal than the first day Jillian had seen her.

The horses began to retreat beyond the courtyard wall just as Ivenna picked herself up from the ground. Fiercely clutching her staff, she aimed it at the horses and sent flashes of piercing, hot light in their direction, but Bella spread her white light into a protective shield around her friends. Under Bella's protective orb, Bella and the Starstone Otter Queen led the way out into the open grass of the castle grounds.

Jillian had long imagined a day when her magical friends would be captives no longer. Now it was here.

If only she were among them!

With the magical creatures now safe from Ivenna and her wolves, the great black stallion reared up, turning his attention to Myrfor. Thunder's massive hooves struck the stones beneath him, sending sparks exploding all around.

Myrfor snarled viciously in

response. He was poised, ready to leap. Just as Myrfor lunged, the black stallion struck the ground again. A bolt of lightning shot out, directly at the huge wolf's face. Yelping, Myrfor stumbled and pawed at his eyes. The stallion shot another bolt toward the approaching Ivenna, sending her body soaring into a castle wall. Then the stallion cantered away.

Ivenna rose slowly and unsteadily to her feet. She threw her fists in the air, furious.

Jillian ran across the room to the opposite window of the turret, overlooking the grounds and forest beyond.

The black stallion had joined the other horses outside the castle. They stood for a moment, majestic amid a swarm of magical creatures. As they turned to gallop off, Bella cast a glance in the direction of the turret.

Jillian felt a warm glow as their eyes connected.

"Don't worry," she said softly. "I'll be all right."

Jillian wanted to believe her own words. But as she watched the horses grow smaller and smaller in the distance, she couldn't help but feel completely alone.

10

*J*illian heard the wooden door rattle. A key jangled in the lock. Someone was entering the room in the turret.

Jillian's body stiffened as the door flew open. There stood Ivenna—and Conall.

Conall's eyes met Jillian's. Then he quickly looked away. She tried to read his expression, but could not.

"Well," Ivenna said. "Where is your great Bella now? Ran off and left you, didn't she? And took all of your magical little animal friends, too. Not to worry, though. They'll be back soon. In fact, *you're* going to get them back."

"I'll never help you!" Jillian cried.

"You have no choice," Ivenna snapped. "Conall here will see to that. You may be able to charm some silly little creatures of the forest, but you hold no power over my wolf pack."

With that, Ivenna turned to Conall.

"It's time to prove yourself, son of Myrfor. The magical creatures will not return to the castle now, even if this wretched girl summons them. They are too afraid of the castle. So you are to lead her to the forest and guard her there until she has drawn every magical creature back to her. I am days away from perfecting a formula that will transfer the creatures' magic to me. Once I have that magic, I will rid this world of those horses once and for all. I am too close to victory to have my plans foiled now," Ivenna ranted.

Conall nodded silently, his expression still unreadable.

"If this stupid girl refuses to cooperate . . . you know what to do," Ivenna continued. "You have until the morning to return with all the magical creatures. If you are not back by sunrise, I will release the pack. They are riled up and hungry for revenge. They will take it out on you as well as the girl if you fail me."

Ivenna plunged a bony hand into her cloak.

"You'll be needing this," she told Jillian with a sneer. In her hand she held the small midnight-blue book.

Jillian's hand trembled as she reached for her journal. The small book that had brought her so much solace now seemed like a dangerous weapon. She didn't want to take it, didn't want to use its power to lure her friends back. She could only hope Conall was truly on her side. If he was, maybe they could find a way out of this together.

"Take it!" Ivenna shrieked.

Jillian had no choice. Her hand closed around the soft, familiar leather.

"Now get out of my sight," Ivenna said, and stormed out the door.

Jillian shivered. As she and Conall hiked deeper into the forest, the air grew colder and colder. The ground they now traveled was covered in snow. Jagged mountains loomed ahead, silhouetted in the moonlight.

Jillian had not dared speak until they were beyond the castle grounds. At last, she broke the silence.

"I'm sorry, Fuzzy Foot," she said. "Sorry I dragged you into this mess. I just wanted to help the others. Please understand."

Conall let out a soft grumble.

Jillian knew her friend well enough to understand what his quiet response meant. He was not angry with her. She felt a rush of relief.

As they reached a clearing, Conall stopped. He looked at Jillian and then down at the journal clutched in her cold hands.

"No," Jillian whispered, thinking of all of her animal friends. "Surely, you don't want me to lure them back here . . . back to Ivenna."

But Conall's gaze didn't waver.

Jillian thought about everything Conall had done for her and the magical creatures. She had asked a lot of him when she sent him to find Bella. Surely he had proven himself. Even though he seemed to be telling her to do something terribly wrong, maybe it was time for her to trust him now.

Carefully, Jillian opened the notebook and began flipping through the pages. Drawing after drawing, creature after creature.

Her mind fixated on the images, and the memories rushed over her in a warm flood. She saw all of her magical friends: tomtommes, twinkle imps, bobolinks, fire spoops, and pipsqueak longtails. Whiffle bears, bubble turtles, tassel mice, rose dragons, and tea leaf pandas.

Jillian reached the last drawing . . . the Starstone Otter. She thought of how gentle and wise the creature had been.

Suddenly, a light appeared in the distance, glowing through the still night. Whatever it was, it was coming closer.

Jillian's heart beat more quickly. The light now blinked through the trees, only yards away. Had Ivenna already released the pack?

A twinkle imp fluttered into the clearing. She was followed by a violet pixie and a whiffle bear. Then, trudging through the snow appeared tea leaf pandas, bubble turtles, and rose dragons. On their shoulders perched tassel mice and pipsqueak longtails.

All of the magical creatures had

returned, flocking to Jillian.

She was happy to see their familiar faces, but she was also terrified. This was just what Ivenna wanted.

Before she could do anything, branches rustled.

There in the moonlight stood Bella. Poised gracefully on her back was the otter, the Starstone glowing softly around her neck.

Bella looked at Jillian, and then at Conall.

Conall moved closer to Jillian.

Slowly, gently, he nudged her with his muzzle . . . toward Bella and the others.

Jillian stared at her friend, sad and confused.

"Fuzzy Foot?" she whispered.

He let out a tiny growl in response. *Go with them.*

"But what will happen to you?" Jillian asked.

Conall did not answer. He just gave

his friend one last glance and bounded off through the woods in the direction of Styginmoor Castle.

Jillian turned to Bella. The great white horse's eyes glowed, full of kindness and knowledge.

Just as you have faced your destiny, so must he face his.

*C*onall entered the castle courtyard at a swift trot. Inside, wolves
stood anxiously at attention as Ivenna
stormed through their midst.

"Conall!" Ivenna said, noticing he
had returned without the other animals
or the girl. "Explain yourself, you worthless hound!"

Conall strode over to Ivenna. His
golden eyes were ablaze with anger. Not
a trace of fear remained in his being.

Facing his mistress, he let out a
growl. The sound flowed from deep

within him. His message was clear. He had betrayed Ivenna—had helped Bella and the others escape—and he was not sorry. He would no longer serve this cruel mistress with her hateful tyranny.

At once, Conall felt free.

Ivenna stood in stony silence. Slowly, a flush of red rose in her pale cheeks. Her eyes narrowed.

Finally, she spoke, her words like daggers. "I hope you enjoy your final moments."

She stepped closer to Conall. Her heavy metal staff echoed dully on the stone floor with each step. When they were just inches apart, she raised her arm with the staff high in the air, ready to strike.

To Myrfor and the remaining pack, she called, "He was always the runt, small and weak! And he still is weak! Isn't he? Isn't he *weak*?"

The pack howled in agreement, quick to turn on one of their own.

Myrfor turned his back to his son in disgust.

Conall braced himself for the impact of what Ivenna was about to do. He was ready to face whatever violent magic flew from her staff.

Ivenna's face twisted in a wicked smile. "Since you think so much of those dear little horsies," she said, "and since you obviously want to be free, I'll grant your wish."

Ivenna threw back her cloak and pointed her staff directly at Conall. A flash erupted from the metal tip, searing into Conall's fur.

He yelped in pain. Then everything went black.

Moments later, a dim light filled his eyes. The sounds of the snickering pack filled his ears. As he blinked, the courtyard opened up once again before him in hazy detail.

Conall knew he must get far from Styginmoor. He tried to rise to his feet,

but he fell. Something was wrong.

He tried again to rise, but slipped sloppily against the stone. He could feel no sensation in his toe pads. His legs . . . what was happening?

Conall blinked again and looked down. Then he saw. His paws had been replaced by . . . hooves. Horse's hooves.

For a third time, he tried to rise, this time managing to stand unsteadily. As the sensation returned to Conall's legs, he realized his body also felt strange. His once coal-black coat was patched with gray and white. A simple saddle was strapped on his back.

Looking up, Conall saw his reflection in one of the castle windows. His eyes widened as he took in his spindly, skinny legs . . . his stubbly mane . . . his familiar, tapering muzzle . . . and white fangs.

He was no longer a wolf, but he was not a horse either. With horror, he realized Ivenna had turned him into an unnatural blend of the two creatures. He was part horse, part wolf. And all freak.

Conall gazed at himself in blank confusion, and Ivenna began to cackle.

"You didn't know which side to choose, did you?" she said. "Wolves or horses? Now you'll forever be caught in the middle. Part of neither the pack *nor* the herd."

Myrfor's lip curled, and he growled menacingly at Conall.

"This freakish beast is no son of mine," he snarled.

"Indeed not," Ivenna agreed. "I'd say it's time for Conall to be leaving."

She slammed her staff on the stone floor and glared at Conall.

"Get far from here, you disgraceful mutt," she hissed. "Let's see how you fare out in the world. I'll give you a head start, but I'm releasing Myrfor and the pack when the moon dips below the mountaintop. I wouldn't want them to catch up with me, if I were you."

Conall found himself in the frozen woods surrounding Styginmoor once more. This time he was alone. He wished for Jillian's company, the face of a friend.

His mind was still in shock, his body stiff and strange. His new legs faltered with each step. Stumbling through the snowy night, he gazed at the mountaintop looming in the distance. The moon had begun its descent in the sky. It hovered now just near the mountain peak.

A fierce wind blew, shaking snow from the trees and piercing through Conall's thin new coat. He shivered and forced himself onward.

Then came a low, menacing howl in the distance. Myrfor. The wolf pack was ready to hunt.

Conall tried to run, but his hooves slipped in the snow. *It's no 'use*, he thought. *How can I run with these ridiculous, clawless feet?*

The pack would soon be upon him.

Gazing again at the looming mountain, Conall made a choice. Instead of trying to outrun the pack on flat ground through the woods, he would climb up the mountain.

It was a dangerous plan. If Myrfor and the others found him, he would be trapped on the mountainside with nowhere to escape. But there was no other option. Conall was certain he could not outrun the pack through the woods.

With a heavy heart and faltering legs, he began the climb.

Exhausted, Conall reached a ledge partway up the mountain. He was climbing a stretch that was sheer cliff. The only way up was a steep, narrow path that wound back and forth along the cliff face. His legs burned, and he had to stop to catch his breath. He knew he could climb no higher.

Suddenly, he heard movement in one of the clearings below. Something was rustling through the trees.

Conall held his breath as he peered over the ledge.

Myrfor burst through the trees, his eyes glowing in the dim light. He sniffed and snarled at the ground, barking at the wolves behind him.

It looked like the pack would continue on through the woods, but then Myrfor stopped. "Be still!" he snapped at the other wolves. "The wind has shifted."

Myrfor threw back his great black head and sniffed the night air hungrily. Then he turned slowly in Conall's direction. Charging at the lead, Myrfor led the other wolves up the steep climb.

Conall could hear the yelps and howls growing closer and closer until at last they were there in front of him.

Myrfor stepped forward. Conall stepped back. He knew he was trapped.

There was only the ledge and the ground, far below.

Looking at the great beast before him, Conall could scarcely believe this evil creature was his flesh and blood. He would rather be half horse than the mirror image of this vicious wolf.

A defiant bravery welled up inside Conall.

Myrfor snarled and took another step forward, but this time Conall did not retreat. Instead he stepped forward. From deep within his gut, he released an ear-splitting howl, somewhere between a wolf's cry and a horse's neigh. The ground trembled, and the other wolves scattered in retreat.

A snowdrift on a ridge above began to quake.

In his mind Conall heard a gentle voice speaking to him.

Close your eyes and leap, Conall.

For once, Conall did not question. As he flung himself off the ledge and into the air, he felt invincible.

Just as Conall jumped, the snow-drift above thundered down in an avalanche toward the wolf pack. There was an eruption of howls from the pack, which cut off abruptly. Then the night fell silent once more, except for the wind.

CHAPTER

12

$\mathscr{C}$onall had been expecting to feel the weightlessness of falling, but instead he was being lifted up on waves of air. He started moving his legs and realized that he was actually *running* on air as he went higher and higher into the sky. The wolf pack and Styginmoor were already tiny flecks in the distance below. *Bella,* he thought. *She must be lending me her flying ability to help me escape.*

Conall looked for the North Star and continued traveling on the air path in the direction of what he just knew in his heart was Trails End. He'd been there only once, but for some strange reason, his heart was pulling him toward it. He wasn't sure how long the trip would take him, but he knew that he *would* make it there.

Jillian and Conall raced across an emerald-green field to the edge of a small stream.

"You win, Fuzzy Foot!" Jillian cried.

Conall nudged her playfully. His new body, like his new home, was starting to feel familiar, although he couldn't call it comfortable.

They stopped to catch their breath. Conall waded into the stream to cool his tired limbs.

"Oh, Fuzzy Foot," Jillian said, looking around. "Who would ever have imagined us here?"

Trails End seemed like a dream to them both. Still, Conall couldn't help but feel like an outsider. Neither wolf nor horse, he was an outcast of Styginmoor Castle and a stranger to Trails End.

This was Ivenna's plan, of course. For Conall to spend his days alone, not truly fitting in anywhere. The thought filled his mind like a storm cloud.

Just then Bella appeared, cantering across the field toward Conall and Jillian. Conall felt his sadness melt away.

He remembered that night, alone on the mountain ledge facing Myrfor and the pack. It was Bella who had told him to leap. She had spoken to him and given him the courage he needed to trust his instincts. He'd gotten there without the Shadow Path—simply by trusting Bella and listening to her voice.

And in all his days here, Bella had never once made Conall feel unwelcome. She treated him with the same kindness as she did members of her own herd. She believed in him.

Bella greeted Jillian and Conall with a flick of her majestic head. The last lingering doubts drifted from Conall's mind like a cloud in the wind. Trails End *was* his home now.

A world away, through the winding reaches of the Shadow Path, deep within a castle colder and darker than Styginmoor, Ivenna and Myrfor faced their own fates. The wolf and his rider bowed humbly before the wrath of one who was even more evil and powerful than themselves.

"Stupid wolfens," an angry voice hissed. "Did you *really* expect to defeat Bella and her allies so easily?"

"Mistress," Ivenna pleaded. "You must understand . . ."

"*Silence!*" the voice bellowed. "It is *you* who must understand. You have failed me. You have failed all Wolf Riders. The next time—and there *will be* a next time—you will not be so careless. If you are, mark my words, there will be grave consequences. . . ."

The great horse whinnied at Jillian. Jillian realized she was meant to climb aboard and ride with Bella. Gently, she hoisted herself up and twined her fingers in Bella's soft white mane.

Bella began to trot, her graceful gait eating up the distance over the ground. Then the two slowly rose into the air, galloping across the open sky.

The wind blew through Jillian's hair, and sunlight warmed her face. She closed her eyes, and her thoughts floated more freely than they ever had. Her mind wandered back.

There was a sun-drenched field. Wildflowers were sprinkled throughout a vast landscape of knee-high grass. In a clearing sat a colorful caravan, painted red and embellished with yellow and turquoise swirls. A line of clothing had been hung to dry in the warm air. Shirts, a dress, cloth diapers for a baby.

On the ground, flattening out the

patch of grass beneath it, lay a colorful patchwork blanket. In the middle of the blanket, a baby with soft red hair cooed and gurgled.

Jillian immediately sensed a connection with the baby. As she studied it more closely, she gasped. It was herself, years ago!

As the thought sank in, she began to see the rest of the vision from the baby's eyes, lying there on the blanket looking up at the sky.

A woman, her arms loaded with fresh laundry, came over. She gazed down at the baby Jillian. The woman had red hair, too, and green eyes that sparkled like gems. Her smile was as bright as the sunshine that formed a warm halo around her head.

This was Jillian's mother—kind, caring, and loving.

A man's deep voice echoed in the background, full of laughter. Jillian's father.

The woman moved out of the picture, and baby Jillian once again lay contentedly staring at the sky. Puffy clouds floated by. Tree branches blew in the breeze above.

Her baby eyes fluttered closed, opening a few moments later as another creature filled the space above her. It was a horse, as white and pure as the clouds above. The horse's dark eyes gazed deep into the baby Jillian's, as if offering a gift.

Bella.

Jillian had known her, years ago, as a baby. Bella had come to her, summoned by the special force inside Jillian that called to animals. Their paths had been destined to cross again.

The memory had lived deep inside Jillian without her even knowing. It had fueled her vision at the castle.

Jillian slowly opened her eyes. There she was, once again in Trails End, racing through the sky on Bella's back.

Only now, a sense of wholeness like she had never known filled her entire being.

The aching gaps in her memories were gone.

At peace with her past and her own special powers, Jillian could look toward her future. She gently squeezed Bella's neck.

"Thank you," Jillian whispered. "Thank you for giving me the greatest gift."

Go to
www.bellasara.com
and enter the webcode below.
Enjoy!

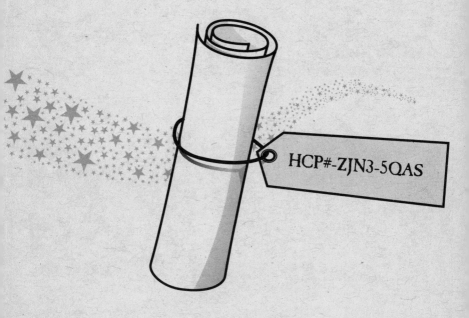

HCP#-ZJN3-5QAS